TEAM HERO

THE ISLAND OF DOOM

ADAM BLADE

ORCHARD

MEET TEAM HERO ...

JACK

POWER: Super-strength
LIKES: Ventura City FC
DISLIKES: Bullies

RUBY

POWER: Fire vision
LIKES: Comic books
DISLIKES: Small spaces

DANNY

POWER: Super-hearing,
able to generate sonic
blasts
LIKES: Pizza
DISLIKES: Thunder

CONTENTS

STORY 1

> *AUDIO LOG OF DR MARANYA,*
RESEARCH DIRECTOR AT THE
ENDEAVOUR OUTPOST.

> *PROJECT DAY 132.*

I HAVEN'T left the lab in months. I
long to feel the tropical sun on my
face, to taste the fresh air again ...
but I can't leave Endeavour yet. Not
when Project H is *so very* close to
completion.

  After all these years, it's hard to
believe we've nearly done it. All the
setbacks, all the risks, all the ...
accidents ... they'll all have been

worth it, if we can just slot the final pieces into place.

And then Team Hero — no, the *world* — will change for ever.

CHAPTER 1

RUNNING THE GAUNTLET

JACK STREAKED through the clear water, propelled by the powerfins strapped to his boots. He clenched his toes and the jets responded, throwing him forward. He stayed as close to the seabed as he dared, swerving around boulders and tendrils of seaweed. Through his Oracle visor, he kept his eyes peeled for danger.

I don't want to bump into a reef shark, he thought.

Ruby kept pace on his right, her dark, curly hair flowing back over her shoulders. Danny swam above, for a better view of whatever was ahead.

The ground rose, and Jack angled his body to jet up the slope. He'd just reached the crest when he saw the glint of metal lurking on the sea floor.

"Capture bot ahead!" he shouted through his mask, sending a stream of bubbles upwards. "Look out!"

What looked like a large metal ball rose from the sand and blasted a

net towards Ruby. She nimbly rolled
sideways, just dodging it.

"Thanks!" came her voice through
Jack's Oracle earpiece. She was panting
a little through her mask.

"Sorry, didn't spot it," said Danny.

"No worries," said Jack, twitching his

legs to rise above a patch of kelp.

The last two weeks had been hard work, but fun. Along with a squad of other students from Hero Academy, he and his friends had been training on board the *Lancer*, Team Hero's high-tech battleship, based in the tropical ocean. Studying navigation and marine biology was really interesting, but he loved the underwater combat training the most.

The powerfins had taken some getting used to, but now it felt like second nature, as easy as walking.

Another capture bot zipped from the right flank, firing a net. Ruby twisted out of the way and glided on. Jack checked the map displayed on the inside of his visor, and realised they were only about a kilometre from the finish line. The only place off-limits was a no-entry zone shaded in red. If you entered it you were disqualified.

They were taking part in the Gauntlet, a test of speed and evasion. The capture bots were sneaky, and fast. Getting snared by one of their nets would slow you down, so Jack was determined not to get caught.

The map suddenly flickered, then went blurry. "What's going on, Hawk?" Jack asked his Oracle. The supercomputer was strapped over Jack's ear and was extending the visor over his eyes.

"Some sort of electromagnetic signal is distorting the map, Jack," said Hawk. *"I'll try to fix it."*

A huge underwater arch lay ahead, covered in rainbow coral. Jack arrowed his body down, beneath the rock formation. He couldn't help grinning at the sheer beauty. Some of the things he'd seen since joining Team Hero blew his mind.

"Help!" came Danny's voice, loud and close in Jack's earpiece.

Jack twisted and saw that Danny

was snared in a net — a capture bot must have been lurking behind the arch. It pulled Danny closer like a squirming fish.

Ruby and Jack shot towards him, and Jack wished he had a knife to cut his friend loose. He gripped the strands with his hands, feeling his super-strength flowing to his fingertips. He tore the net apart, and Danny swam free.

"Thanks!" Danny said. "That was close!"

Three shapes shot past, making Jack's heart pound. But they weren't bots. It was a team made up of members of Green House. They were led by Sienna, who had the ability to change her size from very small to very large. No matter her actual height, Jack felt that she bossed people around like she was always ten feet tall. One of her teammates — Khalid — was particularly easy to spot. He wasn't wearing a mask or powerfins. He had webbed feet and large fan-like fins on his arms and legs. Plus, he had gills.

"Hi, Jack!" he called. "How cool is this?"

Jack always marvelled at the sheer number of gifts the other Team Hero

students possessed, but Khalid was something really special.

"No stalling!" roared Sienna. "We're going to win!"

The three of them zoomed off.

"That's not fair!" grumbled Danny. "He's got a natural advantage."

"It's not over yet," said Ruby. "Come on!" They sped forward.

"Hawk, can you show me what's below ground?" Jack said.

The map showed up the landscape in green 3D, including a system of underwater tunnels. "I think I've found a short cut," Jack said to the others. "I doubt there'll be any bots either. Follow my lead."

Jack turned and swam down, finding a black opening on the seabed.

"You sure about this?" asked Danny.

"No …" Jack replied, "but I'm not going to lose to Sienna!" He plunged into the blackness.

"Activating night vision," Hawk said, as Jack's visor toggled from black to shades of grey. He gunned his powerfins as fast as he dared, following the twists of the tunnel.

Then the map flicked off. *"More interference, Jack,"* said Hawk. *"I'm afraid you're on your own."*

Oh, great! Jack thought.

"Owl's getting interference, too," Danny said, after trying his own Oracle. "Maybe we should turn back. Winning's not everything."

Jack saw that the tunnel forked ahead. "I think I remember the map well enough," he said.

"You *think*?" said Ruby.

Jack took the left, slightly wider passage, and was glad to see it opening up. Jack put on a burst of speed — he just wanted to be in open water again.

But when he emerged he found himself in a larger cavern, his night vision picking out walls coated in lichen and weeds. He scanned around, looking for another exit, and saw several tunnels leading off in different directions. It reminded him of being inside some sort of giant anthill.

The others stopped beside him, floating in the water. "We're lost, aren't we?" said Ruby.

Before Jack could admit it was true, Danny grabbed his arm. His huge bat-like ears were twitching. "Wait, I can hear ..." Danny's head jerked down, and Jack stared too.

On the bottom of the cavern, something massive stirred in the shadows of his night vision. Jack saw plates of armoured shell shifting, and two shining eyes on stalks swivelling up to face them. It was some sort of crab, as large as a car.

"I think we should go," said Danny, backing away.

"You don't say," said Ruby.

The giant crab spread its front legs, and blue sparks crackled along their length, like electricity. Jack realised

that where its claws should be there
were long tentacles instead, slowly
unravelling and reaching upwards.

"Agreed!" he said, but it was too late.
One of the sparking tentacles lashed
as quickly as a whip. Jack tried to

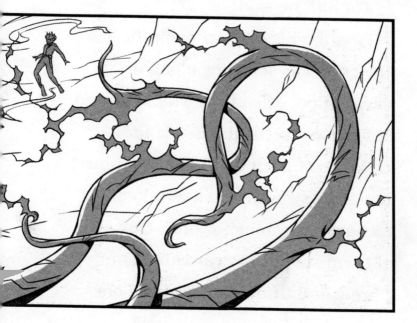

move, but it caught his ankle and a bolt of pain shot up his leg. He tried again, but found himself spinning, and almost crashed into the cavern wall. Peering down, he saw one of his powerfins was crumpled and broken.

"I'm hit!" he said.

Twisting his head in panic, he saw the crab was scuttling along the cavern floor, then up a wall. It moved faster than seemed possible for a creature of such bulk. The lightning tentacles swayed and danced with menace, searching for prey. One of them snapped towards him, but Danny and Ruby each grabbed one of Jack's arms and hauled him out of harm's way. The tentacle lashed the cavern wall, gouging the rock.

That could have been my head!

His friends dragged him into another tunnel, but after a few metres they hit a dead end.

"Oh no! We're trapped!" said Danny. They turned around, backs pressed to bare rock as the mutated crab blocked the other end. Its beady eyes goggled at them, then a muscular tentacle reached into the passage.

Ruby shot beams of fire from her eyes, but they fizzled out in the water before reaching the monster. "It's no use!" she said.

The second tentacle joined the first, like two deadly snakes closing in on three frightened mice.

"I'll buy us some time!" said Danny. "Cover your ears."

Jack and Ruby did as he said, then Danny opened his mouth wide. Even with his hands clamped over his ears, Jack felt the shockwave of sound buffeting the water. The tunnel seemed to shake as the sound bounced off the walls. The tentacles suddenly pulled back as the crab was blasted backwards, spinning into the cavern helplessly.

"Let's go!" said Danny.

Jack, still marvelling at his friend's feat, did not need telling twice. The three of them swam from the tunnel. Beneath them, the crab was already back on its stubby legs.

Which way? Jack wondered. The tunnels were a maze and it was impossible to tell where they'd entered, or where they should go next. If they picked another dead end, they might not get another chance.

Danny started swimming towards what looked like the narrowest tunnel. That made sense — there was no way the crab could follow. With

only one working powerfin, Jack
made an unsteady course after him.

"Hurry up!" Ruby gripped the back
of his suit and hauled him alongside
her. They darted inside.

In places, the tunnel was so narrow
Jack's shoulders practically brushed
the walls, and he was beginning to
think it might be a dead end when
Ruby said, "I see light!"

Jack's heart lifted when he saw it
too, and soon Hawk deactivated his
night vision. They emerged from the
seabed in warm, shallow waters, with
shoals of tropical fish drifting lazily.

"Well, that was ... fun," said Danny.

Hawk's voice came into Jack's ear. *"The map systems are working again."*

"Good," said Jack. He was relieved, but it only lasted a moment.

The map blinked into life, showing the three of them as blue dots. But the sea around them was coloured red, which meant one thing.

"It looks like we've drifted into the no-entry zone," Jack said.

"We're disqualified!" cried Ruby.

Danny groaned. "Sienna and Khalid will never shut up about this!"

"I'm really sorry, guys. That short cut was a bad idea," sighed Jack. "Let's surface. I need some fresh air."

He let his suit's buoyancy kick in, and they rose together until their heads broke the waves. A few hundred metres away, a tree-covered island squatted in the ocean. The sea was dotted with small islands, but this one had odd shreds of mist that seemed to tangle in the trees. Jack was about to put on his breathing mask again when a twinkling light caught his eye. It was coming from among the trees, on a small peak right in the centre of the landmass.

"Look," he said, pointing. The light flashed in a sequence of long and short bursts. Jack knew from

his recent training that the flashes
weren't random.

"That's Morse code!" said Ruby.

Jack knew she was right. And the
message made his pulse race — *SOS*.

Someone needs our help …

CHAPTER 2

DISOBEYING ORDERS

THE BRIDGE of the *Lancer* was an incredible sight. Banks of touchscreens displayed every imaginable piece of information the crew could need. Thermal imaging, sonar, long-range radar, weapons systems, radio signals — the *Lancer* had it all. And the floor-to-ceiling reinforced glass panels gave a breathtaking view of the pristine blue ocean beyond.

Sadly, Jack and his friends didn't have much opportunity to enjoy the view because Captain Harrah, the vessel's commander, was standing over them, going redder by the second.

"Have you any idea how much trouble you caused?" he yelled. "I told Chancellor Rex I didn't like hosting a bunch of kids on my watch. This is an active duty vessel, not a school playground. Not only that, but you've *wrecked* a very expensive powerfin!"

Jack glanced across at Professor

Yokata, their Academy teacher. If he'd been hoping for her help, it soon became clear he'd be disappointed. She stood by, silent and frowning. They'd tried several times to mention the SOS signal, but so far Captain Harrah hadn't given them a chance.

"Sir ..." Jack began again.

"Silence!" roared the captain. The no-entry zone is out of bounds for a reason. Those waters are treacherous. The magnetic signals play havoc with any instruments. The seabed is unknown. Ships that go there disappear *without a trace*. You didn't just put yourselves in danger — you risked the lives of those who had to come and rescue you as well."

"Can I just say one thing?" asked Ruby.

Captain Harrah glared at her, then gave a small, red-faced nod.

"We were being pursued, by—"

"Oh, yes, the rescue team told me," interrupted the captain. "A giant crab with electrical tentacles." He rolled his eyes. "Of all the excuses!"

"It's true!" Danny protested. "That's what broke Jack's powerfin."

"Enough!" said the captain. "I should have you all thrown in the brig."

"Oh, I'm not sure that's quite

necessary ..." began Professor Yokata.

"Who is the captain of this ship?" asked Harrah, folding his arms. "I don't know how you handle discipline at the Academy, but here—"

"Please!" cried Jack, unable to stay silent any longer. Captain Harrah's

mouth fell open in shock at the interruption. "We saw a distress signal coming from that island." He pointed through the ship's viewing panel to the island, which was just a speck in the distance. "We have to send a search party at once."

In the pause that followed, he wondered if Harrah might explode, but to his surprise, when the captain spoke again, it was quietly.

"That is Isla Sombra," he said. "The Island of Shadows. It is right in the centre of the no-entry zone, and it's completely deserted."

"But—" Jack said.

"Completely deserted, and *completely off-limits*," said the captain. "What you thought were signals were just rays of sunlight bouncing off the sea. Now, for the rest of the day you're all confined to quarters. One more step out of line, and you'll be sent back to the Academy."

Jack threw a pleading glance at Yokata, but she just shrugged.

"You heard the captain, recruits," she said sternly. "I'll escort you back to your rooms."

Jack, feeling utterly deflated, turned with his friends to leave. He was sure something wasn't right. *Captain Harrah knows something he's not saying about that island.*

As soon as they were out of earshot of the bridge, he drew up alongside his teacher. "Professor, we can't just ignore the signal, can we? We all saw it — it was definitely Morse code."

Without breaking stride, the Professor replied, "This is Captain Harrah's ship. He gives the orders and we follow."

They reached the door to the students' sleeping quarters.

"But surely it can't be right to follow an order if you know it's wrong, can it?" said Ruby.

Yokata stood by the door as they all entered. "I think you know the answer to that one," she said. As she closed the door, Jack was sure she wore a small smile.

● ● ●

Two hours later, it was dark outside, and Jack was pacing his cabin.

"It's not *right!*" he said. "We're just sitting here."

"I know," said Danny, who was lying on his bunk. "This is the worst holiday *ever!*"

"It's *not* a holiday," said Ruby. She was studying a sea chart on a table.

"You're telling me!" said Danny. "I've not even got a tan."

"We can't just do nothing," said Jack.

"You heard what Harrah said," muttered Danny. "We take a step through that door, and we can wave goodbye to tropical paradise."

"I think there's something he wasn't saying," said Jack.

"Really?" asked Ruby. "Like what?"

Jack scratched his head. "What if the no-entry zone isn't to keep people safe?" he said. "What if it's to keep something secret? Hawk, have you got any information on *why* this place is out of bounds?"

"Negative," his Oracle replied. *"The information is restricted. I can't access it."*

Danny shrugged. "It might just be really, really dangerous, like Harrah said."

"Well, if that's the case, then don't we have a duty to try to rescue whoever sent that distress signal?"

Ruby banged a fist on the table and scraped back her chair. "You're right."

They both looked to Danny. He sighed, sat up, and swung his legs from his bunk. "Something tells me I'm going to regret this."

Jack was already at the door,

peering out. "Coast's clear. Let's go."

Sneaking through the corridors and decks of the *Lancer* wasn't too hard. With night upon them, the other Academy students, exhausted from a day's training, were fast asleep. Only a few of the crew were on patrol, and between Jack, Ruby and Danny, they managed to spot and avoid them.

At the back of the cruiser, several launch boats were poised above the water, ready to be lowered into the ocean and put to use. The night sky was streaked with cloud, but the moon peered out occasionally, and thousands of stars twinkled. Jack checked Blaze, his golden sword made of pure sunsteel, in its scabbard. Danny carried his crossbow with energy bolts, though Ruby had left her mirror shield in the cabin — if she had to go underwater it would just slow her down. Everyone checked they had breathing masks and powerfins, loading the aquagear last of all. As quietly as possible, they lowered the boat to the waterline then leaped on board. They used the oars to row a good distance away, bobbing on the black sea, then started the engines. Jack took the tiller and steered them towards Isla Sombra.

"Jack, I should warn you that you're heading for the no-entry zone again," said Hawk through Jack's earpiece.

"I know," he said. His eyes strained in the darkness, making out the shadowy bulk of the island ahead.

He half expected the *Lancer's* searchlights to come on suddenly, picking them out on the water. But when they were a good distance from the cruiser, he began to relax. The launch cut through the water, sending up a light salty spray.

Isla Sombra loomed larger by the second.

I hope we're doing the right thing, Jack thought.

"You're now entering the restricted area," said Hawk. **"I'm losing contact with the base because of the electromagnetic interference. I can still advise you, but I can't access the Team**

Hero systems any longer."

"Understood, Hawk," said Jack. He looked at the others, their faces pale in the darkness. "We're on our own now."

"Uh-oh," said Danny, nodding towards the rear of the boat. "No, we're not."

A couple of hundred metres back, but closing fast, blue strands of light flickered beneath the surface.

"The crab!" gasped Ruby.

"Can this thing go any faster?" asked Jack.

Danny shook his head. Jack grabbed his sword. He could just

about make out the dome of the crab's shell breaking the surface as it swam after them. It had already halved the distance.

"Let's give it something to think about. Danny?"

His friend had already snatched up his crossbow and loaded an energy bolt. But as he lined it up, the crab submerged completely and vanished.

"Looks like it got scared," said Danny.

"Good work," said Ruby. "We're almost—"

Jack saw the blue tendril loop over the side of the boat, and lost his footing as the whole craft rocked violently. The engine sputtered, then went *bang!* and smoke filled the air. Ruby's fire beams lit up the darkness as they blasted the tentacle. A terrible

shriek cut through the night and the tentacle retracted.

Danny knelt to restart the motor, but it made a choking sound and went dead. Jack glanced towards the island — it was still a few hundred metres away.

"We're stranded," he said. "Grab the oars."

"Oh no ..." said Ruby. "Look!"

Suddenly the water in every direction glimmered blue and Jack gulped. More crabs. *Dozens* of them, all coming towards the small launch.

We're completely surrounded!

CHAPTER 3

LAST STAND

DANNY SWUNG his crossbow back and forth, sending energy bolts fizzing into the ocean. The giant crabs made the water swirl as they dodged his attacks, but gradually they were closing in.

"We're running out of time," said Ruby.

Jack saw another sparking tentacle

reaching for the boat. He slashed at it with Blaze, and it retreated. Dozens of the creatures now ringed the boat.

"They're everywhere!" said Danny. "We need to call the *Lancer*."

"We can't because of the magnetic interference!" said Jack.

Ruby blasted back another tentacle with her fire beams. She managed to scorch the hull too.

And that gave Jack an idea.

"Ruby, can you burn a hole in the bottom of the boat?"

"What?" she replied. "We'll sink!"

"Yeah, great plan," said Danny.

"We need an escape route, don't we?"

said Jack. "The crabs are all around us, but they're not beneath us. We might be able to dive under them before they know what we're up to."

"Or we might get electrocuted as soon as we get into the water," said Danny.

The boat shook as another crab threw its bulk against the hull.

"Jack's right," said Ruby. "We've run out of options."

With tentacles wrapping up over the hull on all sides in search of prey, they quickly donned their aquagear.

Then the boat lurched, and they all fell on to the deck.

"They're trying to capsize us!" said
Danny. "Quick, Ruby."

Ruby's eyes blazed, cutting into
the bottom of the boat. The smell
of melting carbon fibre filled Jack's
nostrils, but he could see Ruby's fire
was weakening. It took a lot for her to
maintain the heat.

Finally, the fire ceased, and she fell
to her knees. "I can't do any more,"
she gasped. The bottom of the boat
was smouldering, but she hadn't
managed to burn right through.

"Move aside," said Jack, kneeling
beside the patch of smoking hull. He
drew back his hand, letting his scaly

fist fill with power. It glowed like gold, and he punched with all his strength. He felt his hand plunge into the water, and the sea began to flood the bottom of the boat.

"Great work!" said Ruby.

"Once we're in the water, swim for the island and don't look back," Jack said. "Ready?"

His friends nodded, and one by one they dived into the hole at the bottom of the boat.

The water was filled with churning crab legs, but as Jack had suspected, they remained on the surface, focused on attacking the boat.

He set off for the island, diving deeper still using the powerfins. After a hundred metres or so, Danny's voice came through his earpiece.

"We did it!"

Jack slowed and looked back.

His friends were right behind him. Unfortunately, so were the crabs, breaking off from the boat one at a time, and swimming in pursuit.

"They've spotted us!" he said. "We need to get to shore!"

Jack's head torch lit up the waters ahead. The seabed here was completely coated in thick dark weeds. Not a single fish stirred — the water felt ghostly and dead. In front, what looked like a tree trunk grew from the ocean floor, but as they came closer Jack realised it was a ship's mast, still hung with slack ropes and tattered sailcloth. The ship itself was overgrown with the same mossy weed as everything else. And as they sped on, more shipwrecks appeared, some old, some modern. They littered the sand like giant creatures laid to rest.

So Captain Harrah was telling the truth about one thing at least. These waters are deadly.

Jack wondered if it was the mutant crabs that had sunk the wrecks, or something else entirely.

The seabed rose, and soon they were in the sandy shallows. Jack let his feet touch the ground, and the friends waded out together into a tiny cove. They detached their breathing masks, all panting hard. Out at sea, in the silvery moonlight, they saw the remains of their launch, upended and slowly sinking beneath the waves.

"If Captain Harrah was annoyed about a powerfin," said Danny, "I really don't want to be the one to tell him we lost an entire boat."

Jack tried not to think about it, and faced inland. The mountain at the centre of the island was much bigger than he'd thought and completely covered in dense rainforest. And he realised that what he'd thought was mist was actually some white stringy substance coating all the treetops.

"We'd better make the trip worth it, then," he replied, and he began to trudge up the small beach. "The SOS signal came from the mountain, so that's where we should go."

The trees looked knotty and impenetrable, but as they got closer

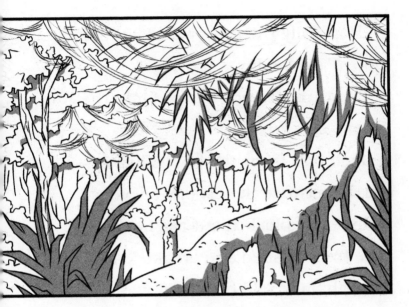

he saw there were ways through.

Then Danny groaned. "No way!"

Jack turned. Back at the shoreline, the first of the crabs was emerging on to the island, its huge legs thumping into the wet sand. The others began to haul themselves alongside it.

"Hopefully the trees will slow them down," said Ruby.

The three friends hurried into the forest, side by side.

Jack had to switch on his head torch, because the canopy above completely blocked out the moonlight. The trees rustled and creaked, and though Jack told himself it was just an ocean breeze, some of the twitching movements of the branches made them look suspiciously like animals. But every time he threw his torch-beam upwards, all he saw was dense foliage.

What if there are more mutated

creatures here?

He kept one hand on the hilt of Blaze when he could.

It was tough going, clambering over giant tree roots and fallen trunks. They had to help one another, stumbling and tripping often. Jack tried to keep his bearings as they climbed up the slope. The signal had come from near the top of the mountain. As long as they were moving higher, they were heading in the right direction.

He heard a crack to his left and twisted his head. His torch lit up a moving shadow. He thought he might have seen a tail, but one covered in spikes. He shuddered. What sort of creature had a spiked tail?

What sort of crab has tentacles?

As they climbed, weariness weighed on Jack. He was struggling to put one foot in front of the other, and his head dropped so he could only see a metre or so ahead. He heard his friends' heavy breathing at his back.

It was because he wasn't looking up that he walked straight into a wall. "Ouch!" he said, rubbing his head.

The others stopped and they all stared up at the strange sight. It was almost as high as the nearby trees, and Jack realised it would have been completely hidden from the beach.

"What's a wall doing in the middle of the jungle?" asked Ruby.

"I have no idea," said Jack. "But the SOS must have come from here."

The wall looked completely bare, though. "Let's split up," said Ruby. "We need to find a way past."

Jack went one way, his friends the other. In places, the wall was covered in moss, but it looked solid. *Built to keep nasty things out,* thought Jack, as he traced it with his fingers.

"Here!" called Danny. "We've found a door."

Jack hurried back, and soon came across the others. They stood in front of a metal doorway. "It won't budge," said Danny.

Jack swept his torch over the door, looking for some sort of latch or handle. The beam landed on a plaque with engraved letters.

ENDEAVOUR

TEAM HERO RESEARCH STATION

"I knew Harrah was hiding something!" said Jack. "This place is Team Hero property."

"So why wouldn't he want to help whoever sent the SOS?" asked Ruby.

Danny frowned, and turned back

towards the forest. His head torch sent an arc of light into the dense rainforest. "I heard something," he said. "I think the crabs might still be following us."

"No way," said Ruby. "They couldn't fit between the trees."

As soon as she'd spoken, Jack saw a faint blue glow. "He's right."

They all stared in terror as the

sound of crunching wood and cracking branches grew closer. Then the dark silhouettes of the crabs' bodies appeared. They were shouldering the trees aside, and tearing others down with their electric tentacles. Smoke rose from the felled trees, and the smell of charred wood reached Jack's nose.

Danny rammed his shoulder against the door then hit it with his hand. "Hey, if anyone's in there, open up!"

Ruby blasted the door with flame, and Jack watched as it grew red-hot, then white. He backed away, feeling the heat baking his face. But as

Ruby gave up, he saw the door was undamaged. The crabs were coming on, a relentless army. Jack guessed they had thirty seconds, tops.

A tinny voice — a woman's — came over a hidden speaker. "*Identify yourselves.*"

"We're from Team Hero," said Ruby quickly. "Our ship, the *Lancer*, is out at sea. Please, let us in!"

"*So you're Heroes?*"

"Yes!" they all shouted at once.

When the voice did not reply, Danny turned to Jack with a desperate expression. "Can you break in?"

Jack pressed his golden hands

against the door and braced his feet against the ground. He pushed but his heels slipped backwards. Next he ran his fingers around the rim, searching for purchase, but the door was almost flush with its frame.

"Please!" yelled Ruby. "Open up!"

No response. The door remained stubbornly closed.

"So we came all this way to help someone, and this is the reward," said Danny. "We're crab food!"

The crabs tore down the last line of trees. There were ten of the mutated creatures, all staring beadily at Jack and his friends. Their blue, whip-like

76

tentacles flickered and coiled.

Terror seized Jack. He slammed his fists into the door, leaving dents in the metal. He'd get through eventually, but time wasn't  something they had. He turned to see the crabs advance.

"Maybe this is it, then," said Ruby, as the first crab launched itself forward. "If it is, let's go down fighting!"

CHAPTER 4

ENDEAVOUR STATION

THE FIRST crab fell back, one leg crumpling as Danny's crossbow bolt struck. But more closed in. Ruby's fire was still sapped from making the hole in their boat. It was now too weak to do anything but slow their attackers. Jack ducked under a lashing tendril, drawing Blaze and ready to fight to

the death. Then he heard a soft click
and a mechanical hum, and he fell
backwards. The door had opened.

"Come on!"' cried Danny, helping him
to his feet.

The three of them backed up as the

first crab ventured inside as well. Jack attacked, slicing off a leg and stabbing at the animal's head. It retreated, screeching, and Jack saw a button on the wall. He hit it, and the metal door closed.

"We did it!" said Ruby.

At first, the inside was almost pitch black, but then strip lights blinked on across the ceiling, revealing a cobweb-filled corridor with another door further up.

"Hello?" said Jack, his voice echoing. "Is anyone there?"

A section of the wall slid back to reveal a vid screen. On it, a woman's face appeared. She had hazel skin, short dark hair greying in patches, and piercing dark eyes.

"Greetings, young heroes," she said. "My name is Dr Maranya; I'm the director of Endeavour Station."

"I'm Jack," said Jack. "And these are my friends Ruby and Danny. We saw your distress call."

The woman's brow creased into a brief frown. "Of course. Thank you for coming to my aid. But, forgive me ... you seem very young."

"We're students," said Ruby. "We were doing training in the area."

"We were told not to come," said

Danny. "This island has been quarantined. No one is allowed here."

Dr Maranya smiled grimly. "Indeed. We've had a ... containment issue. The chemical we were developing leaked and has mutated some of the wildlife."

"That explains it," said Danny. "I don't think I'll ever be able to eat crab again."

"The communication system is down too," said the doctor.

"So is ours," said Jack. "But we can get you out of here if we work together. Are you alone, or are there others?"

Dr Maranya shook her head and bit

her lip. "They're all gone." She blinked.
"I'm injured. I can't move."

"Where are you?" Ruby asked.

"In the control tower. Top level. I can
guide you by speaking through the
building's intercoms. The elevators
aren't working so you'll have to use
the emergency stairs. Just follow the
corridor ahead and I'll open the doors
for you from up here."

The screen went dead, and the
lights dimmed.

Jack and the others set off along
the corridor. The next door opened as
they approached.

"I wonder what happened here?"

said Ruby. "What were they researching?"

"Who knows," said Danny, "but it looks like their experiment got out of hand."

The room beyond was a far larger space than Jack had expected. It was the size of an aeroplane hangar, and filled with small all-terrain vehicles, some with digger attachments, others with chainsaws and cranes. There were hazard suits, large drum containers and forklift trucks. Everything was covered in cobwebs, and Jack wondered just how long ago the disaster had struck. And more

questions raced through his mind.

Why hasn't Captain Harrah or the rest of Team Hero done anything about it? What's the big secret here?

"Turn left for the stairs," said Dr Maranya over the room's intercom.

They followed her directions and

came across more electronic doors, each one closing behind them with a dull thud as they passed through.

They climbed to the next floor, which looked like it had once housed metres and metres of plant beds, all behind transparent plastic sheeting.

"You must be the heroes of tomorrow," said the doctor through the radio. "Tell me, what can you do? Your powers, I mean."

One by one, they told her about Jack's unbelievable strength, Ruby's fire beams and Danny's sonic abilities. Dr Maranya expressed surprise at each, calling them "remarkable" and "intriguing". Jack wondered if she had any powers herself, but it felt rude to ask. She didn't sound in any pain, but if she couldn't move, her injuries had to be serious. At least if they could help her, Captain Harrah might forgive them for disobeying orders.

The next floor was made up of several labs separated by glass walls. They were all filled with computers and monitors, plus beds. It was like some sort of high-tech hospital.

"Anyone else have a serious case of the creeps right now?" said Danny.

"Uh-huh," mumbled Ruby.

"Just stick to the main passage," said Dr Maranya.

As they followed the corridor, they passed a single small window. Jack slowed his steps a little and peered out. From the outpost's position on top of the mountain, he found himself looking down the tree-clad slopes towards the sea. But it was the sight closer at hand that really drew his eyes. Because from here he had a better view of the strange thick strands that covered the tallest branches of the trees.

"Hey guys, check this out."

His friends crowded nearer.

"It's like a web!" said Ruby.

Her description was chillingly accurate. There was an order to the strands — they fanned out in an almost regular pattern. Though the strands were broken in some patches, from this vantage point, it was clear what they formed.

A giant web over the whole island.
Jack shuddered at the sight of it. He
didn't know what could have created
such an enormous web. All he knew
was that they were right at its centre.

CHAPTER 5

MEETING DR MARANYA

THE WINDOW turned suddenly black, like one of Team Hero's hi-tech screens. Then Dr Maranya's face appeared.

"Please ..." she said. "You've almost reached the Command Centre. One more floor. Do any of you have medical training?"

"Only basic," said Ruby. "What are your injuries?"

"It's my legs," said the doctor simply.

Paralysed? thought Jack.

"Don't worry, we're coming," he said. As they headed on, they began to pass odd silken cocoons, stuck among the thick webbing. None was more than a metre in length — too small to contain a person — but he wondered what on earth could have made them.

"Have all the creatures on the island mutated?" asked Ruby. "Spiders as well?"

"The effects have been devastating," said Dr Maranya. "Nothing escaped the compound's corrupting influence."

"What was it you were working on?" asked Danny.

Dr Maranya sighed. "It was supposed to have a medical application," she replied. "We were at the boundaries of human knowledge. We perhaps ... overstepped the mark."

"You don't say," muttered Danny, peering at one of the strange cocoons.

They found the last set of winding stairs. Jack realised the building was like a cone, getting narrower the higher they climbed. It made sense that the command centre was right at the top, with a view across the island.

They reached a door, and it slid open. On the other side, the room was nothing like he expected. It was more like an old-fashioned study, with walls lined with books, and a large desk near a huge viewing window. He realised it was the first room with no cobwebs at all, but there was an odd, slightly sour smell in the air. Dr Maranya sat behind the desk, in front of an array of computer screens.

"You made it!" she said. "Thank goodness."

She reached across the desk and pressed a button on her computer, and the door slammed closed at their backs, making them all jump.

Jack could have sworn the temperature in the room dropped by five degrees. "What's going on?" he said, hand moving to the hilt of Blaze. "Why are you locking us in?'

The doctor pressed another button and Danny collapsed, clutching his hands to his ears and rolling into a ball. "What did you do?"cried Ruby, rushing to Danny's side.

I can't hear anything, thought Jack. Dr

Maranya's eyes wore a gleam of triumph that made his skin crawl, and he drew his blade.

"High-frequency sound waves," said Dr Maranya. "Deafening to your friend's sensitive ears." Ruby's face turned angry and her eyes flared, but

a bolt of white shot across the room, and coated her face. She staggered back blindly, trying to tear it away.

"No!" said Jack. He advanced on the desk, but suddenly his legs shot from beneath him. He saw his ankles tangled with webbing. *Where did it come from?*

He adjusted his blade to cut himself free but another strand of sticky silk snatched it from his hands. Rolling on to his front, he got to his knees, only to feel more bonds wrap around his chest and pin his arms. His super-strong hands were useless, and he fell back, squirming like a fish out of water beside his friends.

Dr Maranya stood up behind her desk.

"Your legs are fine!" Jack cried. "You lied to us."

The doctor smiled. She seemed to

glide behind the desk, as if floating on a cushion of air, and as she emerged, a scream caught in Jack's throat.

"Better than fine, actually," said Dr Maranya.

Jack stared in horror at her lower body. Beneath her tattered, filthy lab coat, where her human legs should have been, was an insect's body, bulbous and sprouting bristling black hairs. Eight brittle legs splayed across the ground, supporting her body.

Dr Maranya was half spider.

STORY 2

> AUDIO LOG OF DR MARANYA, RESEARCH DIRECTOR AT THE ENDEAVOUR OUTPOST.

> PROJECT DAY 179.

AT LAST! A breakthrough!

For so long, my colleagues said it was impossible to give normal humans special powers. They insisted that one must be born with one's abilities.

But they were wrong.

The other scientists disapproved – they're so *unambitious*. But I didn't give up, and my determination has paid off. Phase One — my tests on the island's wildlife — has had incredible results.

But now it's time for Phase Two ... They'll try to stop me, of course, but nothing can stand in the way of progress ...

CHAPTER 1

HUMAN TRIALS

JACK AND his friends had been taken to a bare cell. Ruby was glued to the wall by white webbing. A sticky clump was still over her eyes, making her blind and stopping her using her powers. She struggled to shake it loose, but Jack could see it was pointless.

He writhed in his own sticky bonds. Dr Maranya had stuck him to the wall too in a cocoon of silk, arms pinned so he couldn't use his super-strong hands.

Danny, fixed on his other side, mumbled behind a tightly tied gag. He couldn't even talk, let alone release one of his sonic blasts.

Things did *not* look promising ...

"Your heart rate is elevated, and your blood pressure is dangerously high," said Hawk in Jack's ear. **"I would avoid any unnecessary activity."**

Jack let his body hang limply. His Oracle was right. He needed to save his energy for when it might really matter.

Three of the cell's walls were white concrete, and the fourth was a panel of reinforced glass, with a few tiny holes to let air inside. Dr Maranya scuttled up and down on the other side of the glass. Jack still hadn't got used to her freakish hybrid body. The arched and jointed legs each ended in a black, blade-like claw. He'd never been particularly scared of spiders before, but a spider more than two metres across was a different matter. Blaze, and Danny's energy bow, as well as their aquagear, lay out of

reach in the observation room with Dr
Maranya.

"What do you want with us?" Jack
said to the scientist.

Dr Maranya smiled wickedly. "We'll
get to that soon. You know, even

after I joined Team Hero's scientific division, I never felt like one of you. I suppose it was because I had no specific powers of my own. But I had this." She tapped her forehead. "My brain. I wanted to find out *why* you people could do the things you do. *How* you got your remarkable abilities. I started with animals, combining the genetic traits of different species."

"That explains the tentacles on the crabs," said Ruby.

"Indeed," said Dr Maranya. "An early experiment, combining electric eels and spider crabs. Nasty things! But soon I was ready to put my theories into practice on human subjects. I had to keep it a secret."

"You mean ... on yourself?" said Danny.

Dr Maranya paused, and one of her

spider legs tapped nervously. "Not just myself, no."

Jack swallowed, feeling sick. *So that's what happened to the other scientists ... Are they dead?*

"As you can see, my work has been a complete success," said the doctor.

"That's one way of putting it," said Jack, staring at her transformed body.

Dr Maranya's eyes flashed with menace. "Now it's time for Phase Three."

"Why don't I think I'll like this?" said Ruby.

Dr Maranya approached the glass,

until her breath misted the pane. "You three have such remarkable gifts," she said. "And when I take them from you, I will be unstoppable."

Take them?

"You can't!" said Ruby.

"Hush, child," said Maranya. "It's all in the name of science."

She turned and scurried out of the room on her many legs. The door to the observation room closed behind her.

Danny was grunting madly and nodding his head, as if trying to free himself from the gag.

"We have to stop her," said Ruby.

"Jack, is there any way out of here?"

Jack surveyed the room. "If I could get free, I could maybe break the glass, but ..."

Danny's eyes were bulging as he thrust his head up and down. *He's trying to tell us something ... it's like he's pointing.*

Jack stared at the bare patch of cell wall where Danny was gesturing. Only it *wasn't* bare. Jack thought at first that it was his own vision distorting, but actually there was a strange ripple across the concrete.

The ripple formed into the outline of a person. A girl, who looked about

fifteen, materialised from nowhere.

Danny flinched and Jack exclaimed,
"What on—"

The girl held a finger to his lips.

She crossed the room quickly, and pulled away the patch of webbing over Ruby's eyes. Ruby didn't waste a second before she shot her fire beams at the webbing tying her wrists and ankles. She was free in seconds. She burned Danny free too, and he pulled the gag from his mouth.

"I heard her!" he said, goggling at the girl as Ruby freed Jack, turning the thick strands of webbing to goo like a marshmallow held over a fire.

"Where did you come from?" whispered Jack. "Were you in here all along?"

The girl cast an anxious glance

at the door. "I sneaked in when Dr Maranya put you in here. It won't be long before she returns," she said. "My name is Leila. I was on an internship at Endeavour Station after graduating from Hero Academy. I've been hiding since Dr Maranya went mad. She told Team Hero that a deadly chemical leaked and killed everyone."

A light flicked on in Jack's brain. "*You* sent the distress signal!"

"Yes," said Leila. "I've been looking for a passing ship for weeks. Then I saw the *Lancer*. I thought it was too far away to see my SOS."

"It was," said Danny. "But we were in the water."

"So do you have a boat?" asked Leila. She looked terrified.

Jack glanced at his friends. "I'm afraid not. It was destroyed. Is there no boat on the island?"

"The facility has a dock with one vessel, but I can't get its engines started. Maybe one of you could fix it?"

"Has to be worth a try," said Ruby. "But first we have to get out of here."

"Leave that to me," said Danny. "Move aside."

Jack and Ruby led Leila to the

back of the cell, while Danny braced
himself.

"You might want to cover your ears,"
he said.

They all did so, then Danny opened
his mouth wide. Jack felt the sonic
wave thump
through the room,
and cracks spread
through the
reinforced glass
panel, multiplying
quickly. In less
than three seconds
it shattered
into a thousand

fragments, tumbling across the floor.

"Wow!" said Leila. "That's amazing!"

Danny blushed. "It's nothing, really."

"Let's go," said Jack.

"Wait!" said Leila. "What about the others?"

Others?

"I thought everyone was dead," said Danny.

Leila's eyes dropped to the floor.

"Not dead," she mumbled. "Changed."

CHAPTER 2

NO WAY OUT

"WHAT DO you mean by *changed*?" asked Jack.

When Leila looked up again, her eyes were misted with tears. "I couldn't stop Dr Maranya doing what she did to them."

Jack felt the blood drain from his face. "She experimented on them, didn't she?"

Leila nodded. "I'll show you."

Together, they crunched out over the broken glass. They quickly donned their aquagear, then Jack refastened Blaze to his hip, and Danny snatched up his crossbow. They followed Leila back down the corridors of the compound.

The science student seemed to know the way, and led them around a couple of bends, before pushing open a set of double doors. The dimly lit room smelled like an animal pen, and along one wall were several cells, all with small barred windows. Jack's guts squirmed to think what lay on the other side.

"Maranya's locked the doors and she has the only keys," said Leila. "I can't let them out."

"I can," said Jack, showing her his hands, which glowed gold. He went to the first cell, and gripped the rim of the door. With a yank, he tore it open. Leila gaped.

CRRUNCH!

At first, Jack saw nothing on the other side, then a shadow came stumbling out. Jack

gasped. It was a man in a ragged lab coat, but his face was covered in fur like a monkey's, and he walked on all fours. He blinked. "At last! Thank you!"

Jack stumbled past his friends and grabbed the next door. Barks, clicks and growls came from the other cages.

One by one, Dr Maranya's former colleagues emerged, and Jack struggled

to make sense of what he was seeing.
Jack saw a woman whose lab coat
had burst open to reveal fragile,
transparent wings that fluttered so
fast they were a blur. Another had
a bat's leathery wings. Many of the
mutated people fell into each other's
arms, and thanked Jack and his
friends for freeing them.

"We're going to get you out of here," said Leila. "Follow us!"

She led the group through a door, and down a set of stairs. Jack couldn't tear his eyes from the strange collection of hybrid creatures. Was there any way to reverse Dr Maranya's experiments?

They reached the ground floor of the complex again and stopped in the vast hangar, surrounded by the different vehicles. Leila pointed to a large doorway blocked by a metal shutter. "That's the way to the dock," she said. "We can use one of the vehicles to get there more quickly."

Suddenly, all the lights went out, plunging them into blackness. A cacophony of animal cries rose from the gathered scientists.

"Dr Maranya must know we've escaped," said Ruby.

A dim light spread out from the middle of their group. It was the woman with the insect wings. Her body was aglow like a firefly. Then the doctor's voice echoed across the chamber.

"Escaped, you say? I think not, little *heroes*. I feel you twitching on my web still."

"Uh-oh," said Danny. "Her voice isn't

coming from the speakers. She's *in here.*"

Jack turned on the spot, eyes searching the shadows. Was she there, behind that truck with caterpillar tracks? Or over there, lurking on eight legs behind that digger?

A scientist gave a barking yelp, and Jack twisted in time to see him yanked upwards with a *whoosh.*

"Maranya's on the ceiling!" shouted Ruby.

Whoosh! Whoosh!

Two more scientists vanished.

"Hawk, night vision!" said Jack.

His Oracle extended a visor over his eyes, showing the hangar in shades of green. Jack looked up, and saw the ceiling swathed with vast strands of webbing. It stretched from one side to the other in sweeping drapes, and hanging among the strands were several of the scientists, squirming inside cocoons. No sign of Dr Maranya though.

He pointed. "Danny! Ruby! Can you free them?"

Danny roared, and his blast wobbled one of the cocoons. It broke free, and tumbled to the ground. Ruby rushed right over and used her fire

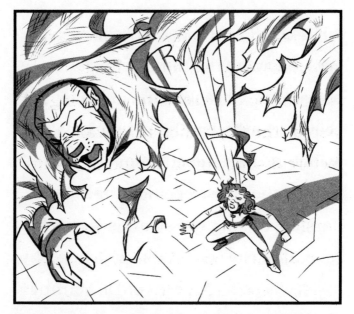

beams to weaken the webbing. A dog-
scientist scrambled out. They went to
work on the others, while Jack drew
Blaze.

Dr Maranya's voice cackled,
seemingly from all around. "Come, my
little flies, let's play a game …"

Webbing shot across the hangar, and Jack only just dodged it. He saw the spider-creature scurrying across the floor, then up a wall, before disappearing behind her white strands.

"She's toying with us," said a scientist with lizard scales, his eyes darting around in terror.

"Stick together and move to the exit," Jack said to the others, who were starting to panic. "If we split up, she'll pick us off."

Danny and Ruby succeeded in releasing the last of the cocoons, and others tore at the webbing to free their colleagues. Jack looked to the hangar door. It was fifty metres away, but if they moved together, keeping a lookout in all directions, they could make it.

Suddenly, Dr Maranya dropped from above, landing on her eight legs, right between Jack's group and the exit. The scientists cried out in fear.

"I've had enough of spiders," said Ruby. Her eyes glowed red and she aimed her gaze at the doctor.

"No!" cried Leila. She shoved Ruby, and the fire beam tore across the wall.

"What are you doing?" asked Danny.

"See those barrels?" said Leila, pointing past Dr Maranya. "They're full of flammable chemicals. If Ruby's fire touches them, they will explode! This whole place will go up in flames!"

CHAPTER 3

A TWITCH ON THE THREAD

THE SWIRLING fire in Ruby's eyes faded.

"That's right," said Dr Maranya. "One wrong spark and we're all dead."

She rose up on her spider legs.

"Duck!" cried Jack, as more webbing streaked over their heads.

"There must be another way past her," said Danny.

Jack searched the hangar, and his eyes fell on a fire extinguisher. "What about that?" he said.

"Worth a try," said Danny.

Leaving the others to free the cocooned scientists, Jack sprinted across the hangar and snatched up the fire extinguisher.

Then he tossed the cylinder, sending it rolling across the floor until it was right beneath Dr Maranya. "You missed!" she cackled.

No, I didn't, thought Jack.

"Now, Danny!"

His friend loaded an energy bolt in his crossbow, and fired. As it was struck, the fire extinguisher exploded in a cloud of freezing white gas, completely covering Dr Maranya's spider body. She screeched and scrambled to get away.

"To the hangar doors!" roared Ruby, leading the scientists behind her, helped by Leila.

Jack and Danny followed on the flanks, looking out. As the clouds of gas thinned, Jack saw Dr Maranya was gone.

Maybe she was hurt by the blast?

Then Danny yelled out and toppled, and Jack saw a strand of webbing coiled around his friend's ankles. He rushed over and hacked through the bonds with Blaze. More flashes of white emerged from the shadows, narrowly missing both of them. He heard the skitter of Dr Maranya's many feet as she crept around the edge of the hangar.

"Help us!" called Leila. "We can't get the doors open."

Jack saw Ruby's fire beams cutting into the metal shutters, but he guessed they were solid steel.

"Try using your sonic blast on the door, Danny," he said.

"And leave you alone with *her*?"

"Don't worry, I'll keep Dr Maranya busy."

Jack saw the reluctance in Danny's tortured expression, but his friend nodded and sprinted away to deal with the door. Jack moved in the opposite direction.

Just you and me now, Doctor ...

His night vision scanned the darkness. The problem was, Dr Maranya could come from anywhere. He let his power flow into his hands, and their golden glow threw out more light. From the door, he heard the boom of Danny's sonic blast, and the echoes filled the hangar. Hopefully he'd break through soon.

The shadows twitched to his left, and Dr Maranya pounced. Jack swung Blaze in her direction and felt the blade connect. The parry rang out against the spider's thick shell-skin. His enemy lashed with a claw, missing his face by the width of a finger. Jack backed off, as more slashing feet darted at him. He fought back with his sword when he could, knocking the legs aside. Then the blade bit into spider flesh. Dr Maranya howled and yanked the leg away, flinging Jack to the ground.

"Don't worry — I have seven more!'" she cried.

Jack saw a leg lift high and then descend towards his head in a brutal stomp. He rolled out of the way and slid beneath the wheels of a truck.

"Come out, come out, little fly," sang

Dr Maranya.

Jack stood on the other side of the truck, watching through the windows. He waited until she was close, then placed his golden hands against the body of the vehicle. Taking a deep breath, he shoved with all his power, pushing the truck across the hangar floor.

The truck hit Dr Maranya and drove her back. He heard her legs scrabbling for grip on the ground, but he continued to push, picking up speed. With a roar, he thrust the truck as hard as he could. It rolled over, and Dr Maranya's body folded

beneath it. She cried out in fury and pain, her legs sticking out from under the truck's upturned chassis.

"Jack! We need you!" said Ruby.

Jack ran towards the hangar door, where the clutch of terrified scientists were huddled. The door itself was buckled, but still standing, and the scientists were kicking and thumping at it desperately. Danny's head was coated in a sheen of sweat from his efforts. "We can't get through," he said.

Jack cast a glance back to the truck. He saw that Dr Maranya was still struggling, and his terror gave him added strength. Balling both fists, he drove them into the misshapen metal with a huge *clang*. The door toppled outwards, revealing a steep mountain road cut through the jungle. The sea twinkled in the distance under a dawn sky.

"Run!" shouted Leila.

● ● ●

It took about half an hour to reach the dock. Jack, bringing up the rear, cast frequent glances back to make sure they weren't being followed by either Dr Maranya or mutant crabs. Fortunately there was no sign of either, though all along the way, he saw swatches of spiderweb strung across the treetops. He knew that spiders used their webs to track and trap their prey. It must all have been Maranya's work.

I wonder how badly hurt she is. Will she be able to come after us?

Leila was right — there was a single boat moored at the jetty. About ten metres long, it was easily large enough to take them all to safety. Along the coastline Jack could see the beached wrecks of several other ships, large and small. Strands of webbing reached from the treeline, fastened to their hulls and masts.

This whole island is the doctor's nest.

They clambered aboard, but when the monkey scientist tried to start the engine, it only turned over a couple of times before going silent. He gave a sorrowful hoot.

"I don't know what's wrong with it," said Leila. "I'm a biologist, not a mechanic."

A woman whose lower body was covered in striped fur like a tiger

ripped off a panel with her clawed hands. After inspecting the workings of the engine for a few moments, she growled, "Someone's removed the fuel injection pump."

"Dr Maranya," muttered Leila. "So we're stuck here?"

Jack's heart fell, and the faces of all the others told him they were despairing too. They were completely cut off. No communications, no food. And with the crabs in the water — along with goodness knew what else — escaping Isla Sombra by swimming would be impossible.

Jack's eyes fell on the carcasses of

the shipwrecks.

Unless ...

"I bet Dr Maranya hasn't removed the fuel pumps from all of those ships as well," he said. "Maybe we could scavenge one."

"Good thinking!" said Leila.

"Owl," said Danny to his Oracle. "Can you find a spare fuel pump?"

A moment later, Danny pointed to a huge modern trawler boat — some fifty metres long — listing to one side, not far along the shoreline. Its deck bristled with fishing nets and winching gear, supported by a crane and pulley at the front near a cabin.

"That one," he said.

"Leila, stay here with the others," said Ruby.

Jack and his two friends ran along the beach towards the stricken vessel.

There was a metal ladder bolted to the hull, and they climbed up one after the other. As Jack hauled himself on to the deck, he noticed a thick silken strand attached to the pilot's cabin. It trembled a little.

"Come on," he said. "Let's find the engine room. And don't touch the web. That's how spiders sense their prey."

Old chains littered the rusting deck. Large plates of metal had come loose in places, revealing the inside of the ship beneath.

"My Oracle says it's this way," said Danny, leading them to a hatch.

They had to duck under or climb over more strands of web. They'd almost reached the hatch when Danny let out a cry. Somehow he'd managed to get his leg caught in some of the webbing. He tugged himself free. "Horrible stuff!" he said. "It's like having chewing gum stuck to your shoe."

Ruby's eyes widened as she stared back at the island. "Oh no!" she breathed.

Jack saw what had caught her eye.
Silhouetted against the slope of the

mountain, an eight-legged shape was moving across the giant web, getting larger by the second as it made its way towards them.

Dr Maranya was coming.

CHAPTER 4

THE SPIDER AND THE FLY

THE HUMAN-SPIDER hybrid moved almost weightlessly across the strands of her web, coming straight for the trawler boat.

"We need to find that pump," said Jack.

"Kestrel says the engine room is the section of the ship that's underwater,"

said Ruby, touching her earpiece.
"We'll have to swim to find it."

"Ugh! That water's probably full
of electric crabs," said Danny. "We'd
have to be mad to go down there."

"We don't have a choice," said Jack.
"Anyway, I don't fancy staying to face
her." He pointed at Dr Maranya. She'd
almost reached the treeline, where
the rainforest met the beach. The
scientists and Leila, further up the
shore, were crying out in warning.

"Good point," said Danny.

He led the way, climbing down a
ladder into the damp cargo hold, full
of crates. The ship groaned, with

strange cracking, snapping noises coming from within. *It sounds like it's about to fall to bits!* thought Jack, as he and Ruby followed their friend. Seaweed and barnacles crusted the inner walls, and the whole place smelled of rotten fish. Jack's boots hit the bottom with a dull clang.

Stagnant, oily water had flooded the far end of the hold.

"Our head torches will be useless in that," said Ruby, her voice echoing. "We won't be able to see a thing!"

But echoes gave Jack an idea. He recalled how Danny's voice had echoed around the hangar when he was trying to smash down the metal door. "Maybe you could use your voice like sonar?" he said.

"Huh?" said Danny.

"Dolphins do it. So do bats. They send out sound waves which bounce back, showing them what's ahead, like a map."

"Great, but I'm a human!" said Danny.

"But you've got your Oracle," Jack reminded him. "You could ask Owl to map the reflected sound. Isn't that right, Hawk?"

"It might be possible," said Hawk.

Danny shrugged. "I suppose this

means *I'm* the one who's fetching the
pump, then?"

"We'll hold the doctor off," said Jack.

Danny nodded and tossed his
crossbow to Ruby. He bent his legs
to jump into the water, then paused,
looking back. "Good luck, guys." He
disappeared in a splash.

Jack and Ruby climbed back on to
the creaking deck. In several places,
bolts had come loose, letting the
plates of metal cladding buckle or
slide apart. Seaweed sprouted from
the cracks, and sand had drifted up
against the edges of the deck. They
were just in time to see Dr Maranya

reach the point where her web attached to the front of the ship. She let her weight flip her body upside down, hanging from a thread. "No one escapes Isla Sombra," she hissed.

Ruby loosed an energy bolt, cutting through the silk thread. Dr Maranya toppled, landing on the points of her eight legs on the tilting deck.

"Nowhere to run now," Maranya said. "This wreck will be your grave."

"If we work together, we can defeat her," said Jack, brandishing Blaze.

"Or you can both die," said Maranya.

Ruby dropped into a crouch and fired Danny's crossbow. The

bolt flashed across the deck, but
Dr Maranya scuttled behind the
pilot's cabin. The energy bolt arced
harmlessly over the beach and into
the trees beyond.

"Too slow!" said Dr Maranya
blasting a clump of spider goo that
knocked the bow from Ruby's hands.

She then shot out more strands of silk that latched on to some of the metal panels, tearing them free.

"What's she up to?" said Ruby.

Jack wondered the same, but the important thing was to buy Danny time. He pointed his sword. "Come out, Doctor," he called.

"With pleasure," came the reply.

Dr Maranya hopped up on to the roof of the cabin, which creaked under her weight. Jack gasped. Using her sticky web, she'd fastened pieces of metal plating all over her body like armour, as well as shards of glass on the points of her claws.

"Just a few modifications," she said.

Ruby shot flames at her, but Dr
Maranya simply shifted and let the
bolt glance off the armour and fizz
into the deck. Then she leapt down,
and came towards them in jerking
movements. Jack stood his ground
and swung Blaze. It connected with
a steel-clad leg and sparks showered
over both of them. Dr Maranya sliced
at him and a shard of glass narrowly
missed his face. Jack retreated as
more legs slashed and prodded. He
flicked his sword up in desperate
parries, hands glowing. Each time
he saw an opening to attack, his

enemy threw a leg in his path. The deck was slick with weeds, making it almost impossible to get a firm footing, but Dr Maranya had no such problems. Her eight spider feet kept her perfectly stable, and she pressed towards him relentlessly.

"I've got it!" came Danny's voice.

Jack saw his friend, dripping wet, emerging from the hold, and cradling the fuel pump in his arms.

"Take it to the others!" cried Jack.

Dr Maranya made for his friend, but Ruby sprayed fire from her eyes, making the metal shielding glow red hot. A beam found a gap in the armour and hissed as it singed her bulbous body. The doctor shrieked and backed off, allowing Danny time to jump over the side of the ship into open water. He sped through the shallows, back towards the jetty. Then Jack saw telltale flashes of blue in the water.

The electric crabs!

"Ruby, cover him with the crossbow!" he yelled. "I'll follow soon."

Ruby nodded, lunged to retrieve the crossbow and jumped over the side of the boat after Danny.

Dr Maranya, smoke rising from her wounds, had recovered.

"You don't stand a chance," she said.

Jack took a deep breath and spun Blaze over and over in his hands. "Maybe not. But my friends will escape and tell everyone what you've done here. It's over."

He ran at the hideous creature, but only made it three or four steps before a bolt of silk caught his ankles and he crashed on to the deck. He lost his grip on his sword, which skittered away.

Suddenly his foot lurched upwards, lifting him from the deck. Dr Maranya hung him upside down from one of the winches by a rope of her silken webbing. He heard the terrifying sound of spider feet and she appeared in front of him, grinning. In her human hand she held his sword.

"How amusing," she said, drawing it. "Run through with your own blade."

Jack closed his eyes, helpless, and prepared to die.

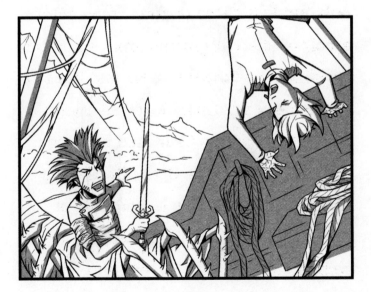

CHAPTER 5

A WATERY GRAVE

THE KILLING blow never fell.

BOOM!

Jack felt a shock wave rip through him, and opened his eyes to see Dr Maranya cry out and stumble across the deck. On the island, a huge mushroom cloud of smoke was rising from the Endeavour Station compound. Flames licked the treetops.

Dr Maranya let the sword drop, her wide eyes reflecting the orange glow.

"My research!" she shrieked. "No!"

As the smoke cleared, Jack saw a huge bird flying from the wreckage. *No — not a bird.* It was the scientist who'd been crossed with a firefly.

The firefly scientist must have detonated those barrels of chemicals to blow up the labs!

Jack threw his body sideways, swinging on the silk rope. He grabbed the cargo crane and clung on, then ripped the bindings free from his ankles. The crane groaned.

Beneath him, on the deck, Dr Maranya snapped her attention from the remains of Endeavour Station. Her eyes searched for Jack and found him. Her blade-tipped legs clattered on the deck as she turned to face him.

"You'll pay for this," she said. "You'll all pay!"

She charged at the crane, ramming into it. With a splintering crack it began to tip. Jack threw himself off, landing hard on the deck and breaking into a roll. He rose shakily to his feet, just as the crane crashed down. Dr Maranya scuttled over the top of it, face twisted with fury.

Without a weapon, all Jack could do was run towards the back of the ship, pursued by the pounding feet of the doctor. On the way, he saw an anchor chain, and scooped up a coil. He doubled back, yanking the links tight and dragging it under her legs. Dr Maranya managed to lift her front legs, but the chain snagged her back ones, tripping her up. She collapsed in a heap, down but not defeated.

As she regained her footing, she fired a blast of sticky webbing. Jack ducked behind the leaning winch and the webbing splatted into the remains of the ship's cabin. The ship rocked, listing over more heavily. He scampered on to the roof of the cabin, using the trawler's huge antennae mast for cover. Bolts and rivets popped and cracked under the strain of the ongoing battle.

This ship is falling to bits! I have to get off!

But he didn't even have a weapon. As soon as he turned his back on Dr Maranya, she would ensnare him with web or cut him to ribbons with her claws. Jack's hands glowed where he touched the antennae mast. He wondered — could he lift it?

"Come out, hero," called the doctor.

"I'm not finished with you."

Jack gripped the mast with both hands, letting his power flow through his fingers. He stood up, straining, and heaved all five metres of the mast with him like a massive log.

Dr Maranya's eyes widened. "Impressive," she said with a snarl.

She bent her legs and leapt towards Jack. Her blade-like legs all pointed at him, each as sharp as a dagger.

Don't miss!

Jack grunted as he swung the mast. The huge metal pole whipped through the air, catching Dr Maraya in mid-leap with a sickening thump.

She crashed back to the deck and
then slid into the murky waters of the
cargo hold. Jack heard the splash. He
dropped the mast, quickly picked up
Blaze, then rushed to the edge of the
opening, peering down. Dr Maranya

lay on her back, legs curled up, while the oily water sloshed around her.

Was she dead?

The whole ship groaned like an injured creature, and the deck began to buckle. Jack almost fell into the hold as well, but managed to steady himself. From a distance, he heard the growl of an engine. The walls of the hold cracked and broke open, and more water started to gush in. Dr Maranya's legs twitched as the water swept her up.

She made for the edge of the hold, like a spider trapped in the bath. Jack saw blue flickers in the water, converging towards her. She spotted them too and her human eyes lit up in panic. "Help me!" she called.

But Jack couldn't do a thing. The cabin behind him collapsed completely, crashing through the deck, and the ship's bow leaned up as the water flooded in. He tumbled across the deck, grabbing desperately at anything he could to slow his slide, then fetched up against the edge. The structure crunched and cracked as metal panels split apart. Barrels and chains tumbled past, splashing into the water.

Jack threw himself over the side,

diving into the ocean. The water swallowed him, and bubbles made it almost impossible to see, but he kicked as hard as he could through the debris, praying he was heading for open water. After a few seconds, he surfaced, finding himself about a hundred metres out from the shore. Looking back, he saw the trawler falling in on itself, swallowed by the waves.

A swell of current caught him like a bobbing cork, and he heard Ruby's voice. "Grab hold!"

He twisted to see the ship from the island drawing alongside. *They've*

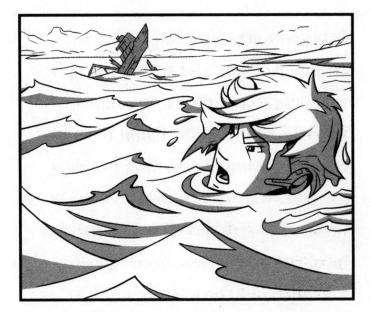

fixed it with the new fuel pump! A life-ring was tossed from the deck. Jack swam over and grabbed it. As he was hauled up on to the deck, he cast a final look back at the sinking vessel.

Dr Maranya did not emerge.

• • •

On the *Lancer*, it wasn't quite the heroes' welcome Jack had hoped for.

"Disobeying a direct order," shouted Captain Harrah, spit flying from his lips. "Breaking quarantine. Stealing a Team Hero vessel. Destroying said vessel. The list is endless. I should have you all slapped in a cell for a month. Court-martialled. Deck-scrubbing. Keel-hauled ..."

"He's going to say walking the plank next," Ruby muttered in Jack's ear.

Jack sniggered, which stopped the captain in his tracks. He glowered. "Is something funny, recruit?" he roared.

"No, sir," said Jack, trying to wipe

the smile off his face, and *almost* succeeding.

"None of you seem to grasp how serious this matter is," said the captain. "It's certainly the last time I will ever allow—"

"I think you've made your point," interrupted Professor Yokata. "Chancellor Rex requests that we handle this from here."

Captain Harrah's brow darkened.

"Rest assured, Captain. They *will* be dealt with properly."

Harrah made a growling noise deep in his throat. "Very well," he said crossly. "If you'll excuse me, I have a ship to run." He turned on his heel and stalked off.

Professor Yokata waited until he was out of earshot, then smiled.

"Well ... you three have certainly made an impression, I'd say. Chancellor Rex sends his gratitude. You all acted with courage."

Jack saw Danny blushing, and pride swelled in his chest.

"Will the scientists be OK?" asked Ruby.

Professor Yokata nodded. "Team Hero HQ is sending medical specialists and science officers. We should be able to reverse the effects of the experiments,

though some of the scientists have

elected to keep their ... modifications."

"And has there been any news

of Dr Maranya?" asked Jack. He

remembered the terror on her face as

the crabs swarmed her and the ship

sank. Though she was his enemy, he

couldn't wish her an end like that.

She was a normal person once, Jack thought. *Too normal. That was what drove her to do such terrible things.*

"Negative," said Yokata. "We have scoured the wreckage, and the ruins of Endeavour Outpost. Nothing."

Jack glanced across at his friends, who looked solemn. It was Danny who broke the silence. "So are we really on deck-scrubbing duty?" he asked.

"I think not," said Professor Yokata. "I'm sure the captain will calm down soon. However, you still have something to prove."

"What?" exclaimed Ruby.

"That you can complete the Gauntlet, of course," said the teacher. "You failed last time, remember?"

"But—" Danny began.

"No excuses!" said Professor Yokata. "Get suited up. This isn't a holiday!"

Jack grinned. The Professor might well be impressed with them saving a group of scientists and thwarting a giant spider monster, but she wasn't about to get in the way of their tests and training! Being a Team Hero recruit wasn't all about life and death adventures. *And maybe that's a good thing!*

THE END

CHAPTER 1

MOUNTAIN ATTACK

"WAIT UP, guys!" Danny called.

Jack pulled his mule to a stop and looked back along the mountain path. Not again! For about the tenth time in as many minutes Danny was yanking at his trouser leg, trying to pull the frayed hem out of his mule's mouth. Ruby had her hands on her hips, watching him from her own mule.

"The stupid thing won't go!" Danny said, red faced. "It just wants to eat my trousers!" He jabbed his heels into the creature's sides.

"Your mount isn't a thing," Ruby said. "She's a she. And of course she won't go if you keep kicking her! You've got to get on her good side."

"I don't think she's got a good side!" Danny said, pushing his sweaty black hair behind his bat-like ears. "I think she hates me."

"Nah," Ruby said, "if she hated you, she'd have dumped you off the mountain long ago."

Danny glanced over the edge of the mountain path, then anxiously back at his mule. The high, rocky path was so narrow the three Hero Academy students had to trot single file. On one side, a sheer rock wall stretched up towards the clear blue sky. To the other, the mountain dropped away so steeply it made Jack feel giddy to look down.

Check out book 9:
THE ICE WOLVES
to find out what happens next!